To Evangeline and Timothy,
who have brought great joy
into our world. Here is a little
in return, just for you.

MASCOT® BOOKS

www.mascotbooks.com

Amal the Thirsty Gamal: A Christmas Tale

Second printing. This Mascot Books edition printed in 2021.

For more information, please contact:
Mascot Books
620 Herndon Parkway, Suite 320
Herndon, VA 20170
info@mascotbooks.com

Library of Congress Control Number: 2020923044

CPSIA Code: PRT1020B
ISBN-13: 978-1-64543-869-4

Printed in the United States

Robert Schorr

Illustrated by Kristina Koontz

Amal the Thirsty Gamal
A Christmas Tale

This is the story of Amal the Gamal,
which is the name, in the East,
in some countries at least,
for a "camel" of course—
not a "pig" or a "horse"—
but a "camel"; you know,
that thing with the bump?
Though, to be more precise,
let's call it a "hump."
Amal had one too and so that settles that:
He *was* a "gamal"—
like the rest of them all.
Except...

1

Except for the fact that his hump was so small,
with practically no room for water at all;
which meant he was thirsty most of the time,
and, out in the desert, that's not a good sign!
But other than that little problem, Amal
was a perfectly normal and healthy gamal.

Well, let's just say "healthy" and leave it at that,
for certainly "normal" isn't the word.
The thought of a thirsty camel's absurd!
Of all the ridiculous things under the sun,
that a camel is never supposed to be,
"thirsty" would have to be ranked number one.
And, probably, even two and three!

Camels are uppity creatures, you know!
They take so much pride in how far they can go
without taking a drink. They don't need a drop.
They can travel for miles and not even stop
for a gulp or a slurp,
or a sip or a drip.
They just keep on walking
and finish their trip.

We're talking about lands that are quite far away,
where the sun bakes down on the sand all day,
with dry, barren desert for miles around,
and water is something not easily found.

When Amal was still small,
about four feet tall,
he'd often hear other gamals in the stall
make fun of his hump: "It's so little, you know!
It'll never hold fluids enough when you go
on your trips with those traveling caravans
out over the desert to faraway lands.
We go a long way, with no stop in between.
And that's the littlest hump we've ever seen!"

And Amal would reply,
"Shall I bring a canteen?"

It was enough to make even a grown camel fret,
but for a little gamal the size of Amal?
Well, he was too young to go on trips yet,
so he still had time;
there was no need to worry,
but let's put it this way:
when it came to the subject of growing up,
Amal was certainly not in a hurry!

But grow up he did! Like every gamal.
Grew up to be about seven feet tall,
and stood just as proud as the rest of the pack;
if you measured, that is, to the top of his head
and not to that pitiful hump on his back,
which, as everyone said...
..was...
..still...
..pretty...
..small!

7

A captain of caravans showed up one day
and ordered the camels brought out to the yard
and said:

"Let's all get ready, we're going away.
The trip is a long one, the road will be hard.
There are Wise Men going with us,
so try to look smart!
Don't slack off…
…or goof off…
…or wander off…
These are 'Magi' you know!
You must each do your part.
We'll be carrying myrrh and incense and gold
to a faraway place where, so I've been told,
some great thing has happened,
some wonderful thing,
or a person, perhaps, some kind of king.
That star in the sky that showed up last night?
And woke us all up with its dazzling light?
Well…they say that it moves!
That it might lead the way!"
Then he turned to Amal and said,
"You're going too! So you'd better get ready,
we're leaving today!"

8

"Gulp!" went Amal.
Who, me? thought Amal.
"Yes, you!" said the Captain,
and in no time at all,
Amal the gamal was dying of thirst!
He'd been thirsty before,
but this was much worse.
"I must have more water,
I'll perish without it.
Why, I'm perishing now,
there's no doubt about it!
My mouth is all dry
and my lips are all cracked.
And making me do this
seems very hard-hearted."
Which was really quite sad,
since they hadn't yet started!
Had not even packed!

That morning the drivers brought out all their goods,
wrapping and folding and tying and weighing.
They piled it all as high as they could.
It was heavy and bulky; it was tipping and swaying,
And that's when Amal the Gamal...
...started praying!

It was a sweet little prayer...

"O Lord of the sky and the earth and the sea,
O Lord of all creatures—and that includes me!—
I'm grateful for all the nice things that you give.
All the oats and the grain
and the grass and the fodder,
but I'm going on this trip
and, if you want me to live...
...please...make sure...there is plenty of water!"

Out into the blazing Sahara they marched,
with the sun burning down and the dunes all a-shimmer,
and with every new mile, Amal felt more parched,
and with every next step, his spirits grew dimmer.
They trudged and they trampled.
They stumbled and staggered,
until Amal the Gamal was looking quite haggard!
There could never be water in such desert places!

But...just as Amal had quite given up hope,
they crossed over a sand dune, and looked down the slope.
And there was a beautiful, splendid oasis,
with plenty of water
and lots of fodder
and wonderful, breezy, shady places!
"We'll settle down here," came the Captain's command.
"But...first thing tomorrow, we're back on the sand!"

That night as the travelers lay down to rest,
our poor little camel was very distressed.
I made it this far and I suppose that's okay,
he thought to himself,
and fretted to himself,
and questioned himself.
But now there's tomorrow and then the next day!
What if we travel for miles and miles
and hours and hours,
and then comes the night
and the next oasis is still far away,
with no water in sight?
Wouldn't that...be a fright!

14

When a couple of camels ambled by,
poor little Amal couldn't help but suggest,
"Suppose we stay here? Settle here?
You know, like...for good?
Wouldn't that be best?
I wish we would."
One of the camels (whose hump was quite large)
looked down at Amal with an arrogant sneer.
"Silly flat-top, do you think we're in charge?
Besides, there's nothing but shade and water here!
We're going to a place where kingdoms are born,
so I have heard,
where for thousands of years a king will be reigning!
The thought of settling here is absurd!
So, if I were you, I'd stop complaining."

There will always be strangers on a caravan trail:
sun-baked, sand-blasted, wind-blown things
that come drifting by,
going the opposite way.
What you, on your trip, call "up ahead,"
they'll flip a thumb and say "back there" instead.
And that's what happened at the end of one day,
while the merchants and Wise Men were lounging at rest,
an exotic old traveler came in from the west,
and pointed "back there" just as calm as could be
and said, "A king has been born in a manger of hay,
it's a strange way to come, if you ask my opinion,
with no palace or splendor or signs of dominion,
but...
...that's what they say...
...a manger of hay!"

"Hmm," said a Wise Man, "wouldn't you know?
This journey gets stranger the further we go."

"And aren't your gifts odd?
If you don't mind my saying,"
said one of the merchants who sat by the fire.
"Do you really consider them fit for a king?
Oh the gold, of course, is perfectly fine;
but incense and myrrh?—I can only presume—
are bound to end up in some temple or tomb!
What, precisely, did you have in mind?"

"We do as we're told; we're the servants of kings,"
one of the other Magi chimed in.
"Royal commands are what we have in mind,
and whatever they tell us to bring, we bring.
Though...yes...
...I guess...
...it is a strange thing."

A stable boy was listening nearby,
just a servant of one of the merchants he was,
whose job it was to unload the camels,
and water the camels
and feed the camels,
brush them and groom them, wherever they were,
and then early each morning,
load them again for the journey ahead,
and that night, he decided to speak up and said,
"I'm worried about the myrrh."

"The myrrh?" all of the Wise Men spoke up at once.
"What's wrong with the myrrh?" one of them roared.
"Who messed up the myrrh?" another one growled.
And then yet another one said with a grumble,
"We paid a good price for that myrrh...sir!"
"I know," said the boy, "but it's so hard to pack,
when these animals all have a hump on their back.
It keeps slipping and sliding and leaning and tipping.
That myrrh is a liquid, I guess you all know.
And a camel? With a hump? Well...
I wouldn't call it the best way of shipping.
One of these days that myrrh's gonna tumble!"

There was quite a long silence after that,
as there by the fire, everyone sat,
thinking and fretting about what could be done,
when one of the travelers rose to suggest:
"What's wrong with the little humpless one?
He's flat as a table, as everyone knows,
but for carrying myrrh? As far as that goes,
I really think he'd be the best!"

"Oh no," said a merchant, "he'll never do.
Everyone knows that, with a hump that small,
he's carrying almost no water at all.
Why, I doubt if he'll last but a day or two."

But now, aren't "Wise Men" the most wonderful things?
They seem to know what the rest of us don't.
They often speak up when the rest of us won't.
And always, they show us the right way to go.
And that's why we have them—didn't you know?
And that night, by the fire, after all that was said,
one of the Wise Men was shaking his head.

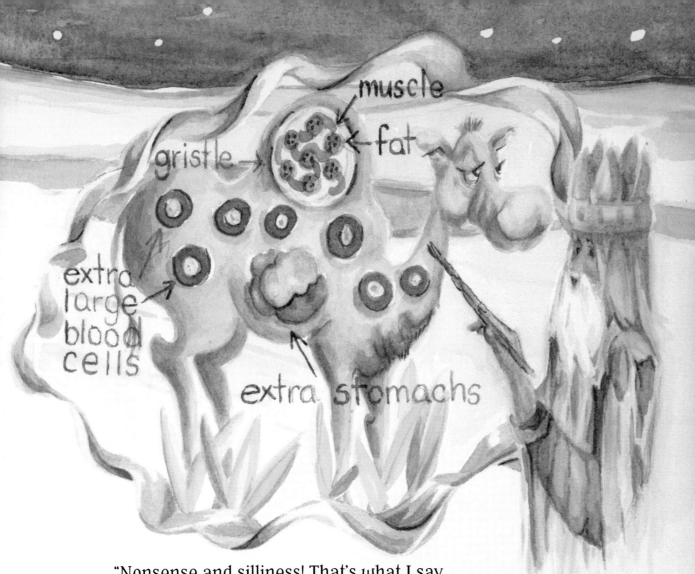

"Nonsense and silliness! That's what I say.
This world's getting dumber, not smarter each day.
And let me urge everyone not to repeat
the ridiculous notions you hear on the street.
You really must try to be more scientific.
I'm speaking of 'humps,' to be more specific.
They have no water. No camel's hump does.
It has muscle perhaps and some gristle and fat,
but no water! None! Not even a drop!
Camels have extra stomachs for that
and extra-large blood cells that hold water, too.
And our humpless friend has all that as well,
why, he'll travel just fine for quite a long spell."

Now, guess who was listening,
while all this was spoken?
Just outside the fire's glow,
but close enough to hear it all.
You guessed it! Amal!
Our thirsty gamal!
Though now of course,
it thrilled him to know
that he really wasn't thirsty at all!
And...
...come to think of it...never had been!

Oh! What a revelation that was!
A Wise Man had said it, and that made it true!
It thrilled; it chilled; it filled
our little, humble, humpless one
right up to the hump that wasn't there;
filled him with joy and pride and delight.
Why!—it kept him awake all through the night!
To think that he'd always have all he would need;
that he could cross any desert now and succeed.
And not only that, but now you see:
he was the one all Wise Men prefer,
if ever they wanted to carry some myrrh!

For the rest of that journey across the hot sand,
Amal led the way for the caravan.
Without all that hump, he was lighter by far,
quick in his step and long in his stride
and way out in front, as they followed that star!

They came to the most beautiful city on Earth:
Bethlehem, of Messiah's birth,
with domes and spires in the deep sky at night,
and the deepest dark blue for the stars up above.
One star, especially, stood over the town,
flooding the streets with its streams of light
that seemed to foretell of a Savior's love.
Bethlehem! Yes! At last they had come!

Amal watched in wonder as the Wise Men got down,
and stepped through the door of a humble home.
And there before a young boy, of all things,
they knelt on the ground as though he were king.
They laid out their gifts in lavish display,
and worshipped there—this holy thing!

25

Later that night, the boy's father came out
to look up at the stars and the deep winter sky,
and there in the stable he noticed Amal.
"Mary! Come quickly. Come look! In the stall!
I think I have found the perfect gamal
for you and the boy on our trip down to Egypt.
Why, he hardly has any hump at all!"
Mary came out with a look of delight.
"Did you say 'no hump'? Oh nice!" she replied.
"It will be such a wonderful, level ride,
and that makes him...just...right!"

And that is how...

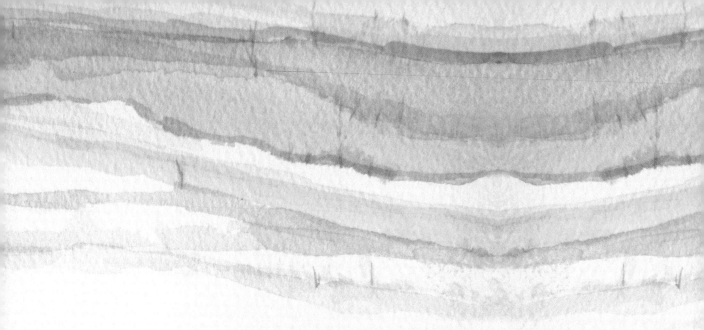

...our sad little...
...helpless...
...anxious...
...humpless Amal...
...the thirsty gamal...
...became the most fabulous...
...famous...
...gamal of them all!

29

Robert Schorr resides in San Clemente, California, with his wife Sharilyn and their family nearby. For twenty-six years he served as Senior Pastor at Calvary Chapel Old Towne in Orange, California. Prior to that, they lived in Asia for seventeen years. He is devoted to his Savior, to Sharilyn, his children, flying, hiking, fly-fishing, Chinese, and writing. He loves any story that makes someone special, and he knew, a long time ago, that little Amal had one to tell.

Kristina Koontz has lived with her husband John in Orange, California, for the past forty-eight years. The artwork in this book about Amal is lovingly dedicated to her grandchildren: Casey, Frances, Sam, and Georgia.

www.themorningfrigate.com